JUN 2010
W9-BPJ-385

Published by
PEACHTREE PUBLISHERS
1700 Chattahoochee Avenue
Atlanta, Georgia 30318-2112
www.peachtree-online.com

Text and illustrations copyright © 2009 by Sebastien Braun

First published in paperback in Great Britain by HarperCollins Children's Books in 2009
First United States edition published by Peachtree Publishers in 2010

All rights reserved. No part of this publication may be reproduced,
stored in a retrieval system, or transmitted in any form or by any means—
electronic, mechanical, photocopy, recording, or any other—except for brief quotations
in printed reviews, without the prior permission of the publisher.

illustrations created in india ink, markers, and colored pencil

10 9 8 7 6 5 4 3 2 1

Printed and bound in October 2009 by RR Donnelley in Guangdong Province, China

Library of Congress Cataloging-in-Publication Data

Braun, Sebastien.
Back to bed, Ed! / written and illustrated by Sebastien Braun. -- 1st U.S. ed.
p. cm.
Summary: Ed the mouse will not sleep in his own bed, until eventually his exasperated and tired parents find a way to keep him from joining them in the middle of the night.
ISBN: 978-1-56145-518-8 / 1-56145-518-0
[1. Bedtime--Fiction. 2. Sleep--Fiction. 3. Mice--Fiction.] i. Title.
PZ7.B73779Bac 2010
[E]--dc22
2009024990

Back to Bed, Ed!

by Sebastien Braun

PEACHTREE
ATLANTA

Every night Ed loved getting ready for bed.

He played games with Dad,

clip
clop

had a drink,

sip sip

and cleaned his teeth.

brush
brush

He had a bubbly bath,

splish
splash

a story with Mom,

then, all tucked in bed,

kiss kiss
night night

sleep tight!

click
Ed LOVED
going to bed...

but Ed **HATED** staying in bed...

tip toe tip toe...

"Dad! It's too dark in my room."

"Back to bed, Ed," grumbled Dad.

But Ed didn't go back to his bed,

and Dad didn't get much sleep that night.

The next morning Dad said,

"Stay in your own bed, Ed.

You're a BIG mouse now."

But later that night,

"Mom! There are
MONSTERS in
my bedroom!"

"Back to bed, Ed," groaned Mom.

But Ed didn't go back to his bed.
Mom and Dad didn't get much sleep that night.

The next morning they slept through the alarm.
Dad was late for work.

Ed was late for preschool.

And so it went on, night after night Ed left his bed.

they shouted.

Mom and Dad had had enough!

The next morning they came up with a plan...

That night when Ed went to Mom and Dad's bedroom, the door was shut. He couldn't go in.

Poor Ed didn't know what to do.

Dad came out.

"Come on, Ed, back to bed!" he said.

"The night light is on,
you've got your friend.
There's no need to be scared.
You're a big mouse now."

But Ed didn't stay in bed. He got up and found

Now he had all
his little friends
around him.

"There's no need
to be scared,"
he said,
"I'm here now."

After that Ed always slept in his own bed,

and everyone got
a good night's sleep...

ZZZZZZZZz

ZZZZZZZZZ

Well, not quite everyone!

AAAHHH!

Sleep tight, Ed!